A Letter to Santa Claus

Story by Rose Impey
Pictures by Sue Porter

Delacorte
Press

DELACORTE PRESS/NEW YORK

For
Charlotte
x x x x

21512

LIBRARY OF CONGRESS
Library of Congress Cataloging-in-Publication Data
Impey, Rose.
A letter to Santa Claus
story by Rose Impey;
pictures by Sue Porter.
Summary: Charlotte mistakenly sends the wrong
Christmas list to Santa but the results prove beneficial to
the starving animals outside her home.
ISBN 0-385-29714-9
[1. Christmas – Fiction.]   I. Porter, Sue, ill.   II. Title.
PZ7.I344Le 1989
[E] – dc19

Published by
Delacorte Press
Bantam Doubleday Dell Publishing Group Inc.
666 Fifth Avenue
New York, New York 10103

This work was originally published in Great Britain by
Orchard Books as A LETTER TO FATHER CHRISTMAS.

Manufactured in Belgium
November 1989

10 9 8 7 6 5 4 3 2 1

The place where Charlotte lived was too small even to be called a village.

There were no other children to play with, except Ben, of course, but he was still a baby. So Charlotte was quite used to spending time alone. Often she liked to draw, or dress up, or watch television. Or she might go out into the backyard and talk to her friends the donkey and the stray cat who sometimes prowled the flower beds looking for birds.

But most of all Charlotte liked to write.

Sometimes Charlotte wrote:

Bread
carrots
fish
Nuts
Milk
Hot water bottle

Or she wrote:

Charlotte Hall
7 Warren Lane
East Kilby, N.J.
00321

Once she even wrote:

Mrs. Hall,
    You need a new
washer on your
    faucet – will bring
one tomorrow.
            Mr. Pipes

Charlotte didn't know that was what she had written
because she couldn't read yet. But she could write
beautifully. She copied anything she could find and she
decorated her writing with tiny drawings.

Today Charlotte was writing something very special – her letter to Santa Claus. She copied carefully from Mom's writing.

Dear Santa Claus,
I am writing to tell you what I would like in my stocking. When you come to my house on Christmas Eve don't look for me in my bedroom because Grandma and Grandad will be there. I will be in Ben's room (next to the bathroom). Ben is too small to write his own letter so I have put some things for him on my list. Also would you bring me a surprise? I like surprises best of all.
Lots of love, Miss Charlotte Ruth Hall. X

And then, since it was such a long letter, she copied out her Christmas list on a separate piece of paper.

Just as she finished Mom said, "It'll be time for supper soon, Charlie. Tidy up, please."

But unfortunately Charlotte didn't tidy up. Although she did very neat writing, she wasn't always tidy in other ways. Sometimes there was so much clutter on her table that she couldn't even find room to write. Today a pile of paper spilled over onto the floor and that was how Charlotte came to make her terrible mistake.

Supper was always early on Tuesdays because Mom went out to an evening class. While she got ready, Charlotte and Dad bathed Ben and put him to bed. Then Charlotte watched television while Dad slept in the big chair. Later, when he woke, he played all Charlotte's favorite games and let her stay up much later than usual.

As Mom left she whispered, "Ask Dad to mail your letter. Why don't you put it in the envelope?" Then she dashed out to the car, blowing lots of kisses because she didn't have time to stop for a real one.

Charlotte looked at her lovely pieces of writing heaped up on top of her table. She picked out her special letter, folding it carefully, as she had seen Mom do, and running her finger down the fold. She slid it into the envelope, then licked the flap, all the way up one side and down the other.

Just in time she remembered her present list. She sorted through the pile to find it. There were lots of lists and they all looked the same to her.

"This must be it," she thought, sliding it in with her letter. But it wasn't. Her list had fallen on the floor. It was lying at her feet right now, but she didn't realize that. Too late she pressed the flap down with her fist. Then, to make sure, she sat on it until it was truly stuck.

When Dad woke up Charlotte climbed onto his knee and held out the letter.

"Thank you," said Dad. "Is that for me?"

"No, silly," she said. "It's my letter to Santa Claus."

"Well, it doesn't say so," said Dad. And he showed her how to address it.

to Santa Claus
I, Northpole Lane,
Frostbite,
The Far North,
000 10

"Now can we send it?" Charlotte asked.

"Okay," said Dad. "You sit back while I mail it up the chimney."

Then Dad poked up the fire until there was a strong draft. When he held the letter for a moment above the flames Charlotte caught her breath. She felt sure it would burn. But it didn't.

When Dad let go it flew
straight up the chimney and out
into the dark night sky. Charlotte
raced to the window to watch it,
but the letter had already
disappeared. It was far away on
its journey to Santa.

When Santa Claus opened Charlotte's letter his first thought was, "Now, that's what I call beautiful writing." But when he came to the list he stopped and read it more carefully.

"This is very odd," he said, pulling at his beard and curling it around his finger.

Santa Claus was used to being asked for all sorts of strange things, but he had never been sent a list of presents quite like this.

"Why, it looks more like somebody's shopping list," he thought. And, of course, that's exactly what it was.

From then on Mom was even more busy than usual. Grandma and Grandad arrived and the preparations for Christmas really began.

For Charlotte the next few days were a strange mixture. She felt like laughing one minute and crying the next.

Everyone else was very busy, but Charlotte couldn't settle down.

One morning she wandered around the house and leaned against a window, sucking her thumb. It was then that she saw the first teasing flakes of snow, there one minute, disappeared the next. She stared hard, willing it to fall faster.

"Come on," she whispered. "Snow!"

And soon it was snowing heavily and it kept on snowing all day and through the night. By morning there was a good thick coating, curved and soft. Charlotte watched the birds landing on the lawn. She saw them searching for the last few berries on the holly bushes.

She waved to her friend the donkey who lived in the farmer's field at the back of the yard. She wished she could stroke him and brush the snow off his sad face. But more than that she wished she could bring him in out of the cold.

Later she tapped on the glass to the stray cat. He was on the lookout for any sparrows too dazzled by the whiteness to see him coming. Charlotte didn't want him to eat the birds.

"But what else will he eat?" she wondered.

That night when Charlotte went to bed she peeped out and watched the snow swirling around the house. She thought about her friends the animals out there in the cold with so little to eat. For quite a long time Charlotte couldn't get to sleep because she was so worried about them.

So on Christmas Eve morning Charlotte was tired and quieter than usual.

"I hope you're not going to be sick for Christmas," said Mom.

But Charlotte wasn't sick, she was still worrying about the animals. Several times that day she tried to get someone to stop what they were doing and give her some food for them. But everyone said the same thing.

"Ask me later, sweetheart. You can see I'm busy right now."

And they went on being busy all day, up until the evening.

When the work was finally done, everyone came and sat quietly together around the fire while Grandma read Charlotte the Christmas story. And at last it was time for bed. Charlotte left cookies and a glass of milk for Santa and hung up her stocking. Then she knew that after all the waiting, Christmas was really here.

She lay in bed, too excited to sleep, wondering what she would find in her stocking when she woke in the morning. Suddenly she remembered the birds and animals; she still hadn't fed them. Charlotte didn't know what to do. She felt so sad.

A large tear plopped onto her pillow. She wondered if Santa ever brought anything for the animals. If she were Santa she would. Charlotte sucked her thumb. Now she didn't feel excited; she felt rather unhappy.

But by midnight, when Santa Claus tiptoed into her room, Charlotte was fast asleep and dreaming. He leaned over to have a look at her. He was particularly interested to see this little girl who had sent him such an unusual Christmas list.

"I hope you won't be disappointed," he whispered.

On Christmas morning it was just light when
Charlotte woke. She crept out of bed to find her
stocking. It was full and very heavy. But, even before she
opened it, she drew back the curtains. She looked out
onto the garden, hoping to see her animal friends. It had
stopped snowing at last. Everything was icy cold and
sparkling. Only the birds were awake, cutting clean,
arrow-shaped tracks across the lawn.

 Charlotte crept back into her warm bed and pulled her stocking onto her knee. She took out the first parcel. It was an unusual shape. She felt it. Her fingers pressed into the sides, which were soft and spongy. She took out the next present and shook it. There was a funny slopping noise. And the next one had a strange smell.

Charlotte began to open them. She couldn't believe her eyes. They were not the toys and books she had expected. They were far more unusual presents than that. She unwrapped them one by one . . .

bread . . .

carrots . . .

fish . . .

nuts . . .

milk . . .

and a hot water bottle.

It was just as if Santa had been able to read her mind. He'd brought her exactly what she needed.

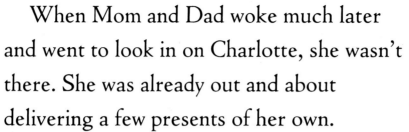

When Mom and Dad woke much later
and went to look in on Charlotte, she wasn't
there. She was already out and about
delivering a few presents of her own.

And Santa hadn't forgotten Charlotte's surprise. At the bottom of her stocking was the perfect present for a little girl who liked to look after animals.

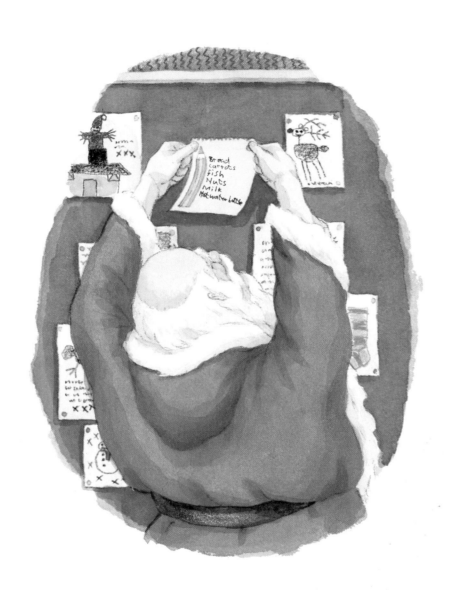